MY
NO, NO,
NO
DAY!

To Anna Christophersen
Best wishes,
Rebecca

VIKING

Published by Penguin Group

Penguin Young Readers Group, 345 Hudson Street, New York, New York 10014, U.S.A.

Penguin Group (Canada), 90 Eglinton Avenue East, Suite 700, Toronto, Ontario, Canada M4P 2Y3

(a division of Pearson Penguin Canada Inc.)

Penguin Books Ltd, 80 Strand, London WC2R 0RL, England

Penguin Ireland, 25 St Stephen's Green, Dublin 2, Ireland (a division of Penguin Books Ltd)

Penguin Group (Australia), 250 Camberwell Road, Camberwell, Victoria 3124, Australia

(a division of Pearson Australia Group Pty Ltd)

Penguin Books India Pvt Ltd, 11 Community Centre, Panchsheel Park, New Delhi – 110 017, India

Penguin Group (NZ), 67 Apollo Drive, Rosedale, Auckland 0632, New Zealand

(a division of Pearson New Zealand Ltd.)

Penguin Books (South Africa) (Pty) Ltd, 24 Sturdee Avenue, Rosebank, Johannesburg 2196, South Africa

Penguin Books Ltd, Registered Offices: 80 Strand, London WC2R 0RL, England

First published in the U.K. in 2012 by Jonathan Cape, an imprint of Random House Children's Books
First published in the U.S.A. in 2012 by Viking, a division of Penguin Young Readers Group

3   5   7   9   10   8   6   4

LIBRARY OF CONGRESS CATALOGING-IN-PUBLICATION DATA IS AVAILABLE
ISBN: 978-0-670-01405-7
Special Markets ISBN 978-0-670-01536-8
Manufactured in China

This Imagination Library edition is published by Penguin Young Readers, a division
of Penguin Random House, exclusively for Dolly Parton's Imagination Library,
a not-for-profit program designed to inspire a love of reading and learning, sponsored
in part by The Dollywood Foundation. Penguin's trade editions of this work are
available wherever books are sold.

MY NO, NO, NO DAY!

Rebecca Patterson

BELLAS ROOM

KEEP OUT BoB

Viking

An Imprint of Penguin Group (USA) Inc.

Yesterday I woke up and Bob was crawling around **MY ROOM** licking **MY JEWELRY** . . .

So I shouted,

GET OUT OF MY ROOM!

And that was the start of **MY NO, NO, NO DAY.**

Then I came downstairs and I saw **THAT EGG**.
I cried and cried and said,

I CAN'T EAT THAT!

And Mommy said, "You could eat it last week.
Look at Bob eating his mashed banana."

After the **TERRIBLE EGG** I didn't like my shoes
either. So I took them off all by myself, shouting,

NO SHOES!

And then we had to go shopping and Mommy said,
"Please stop wriggling, Bella."
But I couldn't stop wriggling and in the end I shouted,

GET ME OUT!

Mommy said, "You will give Bob an earache. And you are giving *me* a headache."

And Bob poked me and said, **"ear."**

At lunchtime Sasha and her mommy came to play and to have some peanut butter and grapes and a cookie. But . . .

MY COOKIE BROKE!

Then I couldn't play nicely and I kept saying,

NO! YOU CAN'T BE PRINCESSES!

And in the end Sasha and her mommy went home.

In the afternoon it was my ballet lesson. I said,

BALLET IS TOOo

ITCHY!

But I was very loud, and Mrs. Clark stopped playing the piano and
Miss Louisa said, "Dear, oh dear, perhaps you should sit in the corner then."

On the way home we met the lady who lives next door
and she said that Bob was the sweetest thing she'd seen
all day, and then she said, "And how is Bella?"

I was a long way behind so I had to shout,

I HAVE A HURTING FOOT!

And Mommy said could I keep my voice down and could I **PLEASE** stop lying on the sidewalk.

Then it was time for my supper and my bath.
But those peas were

TOO HOT!

And our bath was **TOO COLD!**

And I was

TOO WET!

And it was

TOO MINTY!

After that I rolled and rolled and said,

NO BED NO NO

NO NO BED NO NO!

And Mommy said, "Well, I think someone needs to go to bed."

But I rolled all over my room
and then I rolled into Bob's room
and I said,

BED IS FOR BABIES!

And then I yawned
a little yawn.

Then I crawled into my
room, and Mommy said,
"Who wants a story?"

And I said,

NOBODY!

But she came into my room anyway and we cuddled up
and had my best story about fairies and cake.

YAWN...

I yawned again and I said, very quietly,

"Today was a very bad day, Mommy. Sorry."

And she kissed me good night and said,
"I know. We all have those days sometimes,
but perhaps you will be more
cheerful tomorrow!"

And . . .

I WAS! I WAS!
I was cheerful . . .

ALL DAY LONG!